W9-DAD-302

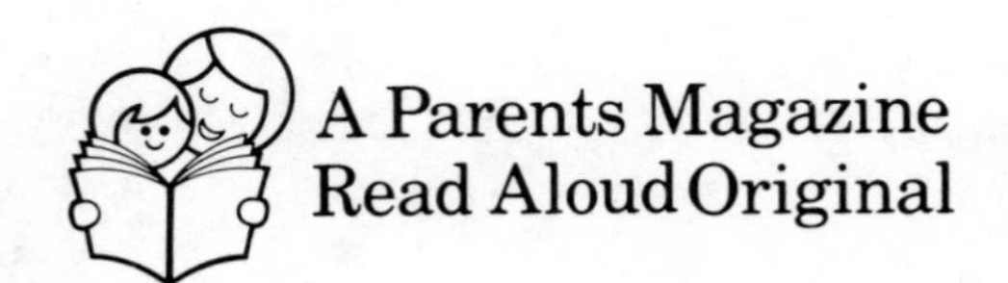
A Parents Magazine
Read Aloud Original

BREAD AND HONEY

A

FRANK ASCH

Bear Story

Parents Magazine Press ✻ New York

Printed in the United States of America
10 9 8 7 6 5 4

Library of Congress Cataloging in Publication Data
Asch, Frank. Bread and honey.
Adapted from the author's Monkey face.
SUMMARY: Ben paints a picture of his mother, with a little help from Owl, Rabbit, Alligator, Elephant, Lion, and Giraffe.
[1. Painting—Fiction. 2. Mothers and sons—Fiction. 3. Animals—Fiction.]
I. Asch, Frank. Monkey face. II. Title.
PZ7.A778Br [E] 81-16893
ISBN 0-8193-1077-8 AACR2
ISBN 0-8193-1078-6 (Lib. bdg.)

To Tracy,
Shannon,
and Tina

One morning when Ben was
getting ready for school,
his mother took a loaf
of fresh bread out of the oven.

"Can I have a piece?" asked Ben.

"The bread is too hot now,"
said his mother.
"But you can have some
when you get home."

"With honey on top?" asked Ben.
"Yes," said his mother,
"with lots of honey on top."

"Okay," said Ben
and he hurried off to school.

That day, Ben painted
a picture of his mother.

When the bell rang,
he decided to take it home.

On the way, he stopped
to show the picture to Owl.

"I love it," said Owl.
"But you made the eyes too small."

"I have my paintbox with me,"
said Ben.
"Maybe I can fix that."

"Fine work!" said Owl.

At the riverbank, Ben showed the picture to Alligator.

"I just love it!" said Alligator. "But the mouth needs to be much, much bigger!"

"How's that?" asked Ben.
"Much better!" said Alligator.

A little way down the path,
Ben met Rabbit and
showed her the picture.
"I love it!" said Rabbit.
"But the ears are too short."

"Oh, that's easy to fix,"
said Ben.

"How's that?" asked Ben.
"Wonderful," said Rabbit.

When Ben showed Elephant
his picture, Elephant said,
"I love it, but the nose
is too small."

Once again, Ben took
out his paints.

Peas

"How's that?" asked Ben.
"Unforgettable!" said Elephant.

Then Ben showed his picture to Lion.

"I love it," said Lion.
"But you forgot a fluffy mane."

"How's that?" asked Ben.
"A picture to be proud of,"
said Lion.

When Ben was almost home,
he saw Giraffe and
showed him his picture.

"I just love it,"
said Giraffe.
"But the neck is too short."

"How's that?" asked Ben.
"Perfect," said Giraffe.

Ben ran the rest
of the way home.

When he got there
he said to his mother,
"Look what I made—
a picture of you!"

"I love it!" said his mother.
"Just the way it is?" asked Ben.

"Just the way it is," said his mother.
And she hung it on the refrigerator.

Then she gave Ben a thick slice
of homemade bread with
lots of honey on top.

✲ About the Author ✲

FRANK ASCH is the award-winning author/artist of many well-loved picture books. He is known for his warm and funny stories for young children. His first two Bear Books for Parents—*Sandcake* and *Popcorn*—became immediate favorites with our readers.

Aside from writing and illustrating picture books, Mr. Asch has taught in a Montessori school and created his own children's theater productions.

Mr. Asch, his wife, and their young son live in Woodstock, Connecticut.